THE
GOOD-BYE
BOOK

by
Judith Viorst

illustrated
by Kay Chorao

Aladdin Paperbacks

CHILDREN'S BOOKS BY JUDITH VIORST

Sunday Morning
Alexander and the Terrible, Horrible,
No Good, Very Bad Day
My Mama Says There Aren't Any Zombies,
Ghosts, Vampires, Creatures, Demons,
Monsters, Fiends, Goblins, or Things
Rosie and Michael
The Tenth Good Thing About Barney
Alexander, Who Used to Be Rich Last Sunday
If I Were in Charge of the World and other worries
I'll Fix Anthony
The Good-Bye Book

Aladdin Paperbacks
An imprint of Simon & Schuster Children's Publishing Division
1230 Avenue of the Americas
New York, New York 10020

Type set by V & M Graphics, New York City
Printed and bound in the U.S.A.
Typography by Mary Ahern

10   9   8   7   6   5   4   3

Library of Congress Cataloging-in-Publication Data

Viorst, Judith.   The good-bye book.

SUMMARY: A child, on the verge of being left
behind by parents who are going out for the evening,
comes up with a variety of pleas and excuses.
[1. Separation anxiety—Fiction.   2. Parent and child
—Fiction]   I. Chorao, Kay, ill.   II. Title.
PZ7.V816Go   1988   [E]   87-1778
ISBN 0-689-31308-X
0-689-71581-1 (pbk)

Don't go.
I don't want you to go.
I don't want you to go to
a French restaurant and leave
me home. I want you to
go to McDonald's and take
me with you.

I'll even go to the French restaurant.

No I won't have fun with the baby-sitter.
I hate baby-sitters. They could make you
eat vegetables.

They could make you only watch the TV programs *they* want to watch.

They could make you go to the bathroom before you go to bed even when you don't have to.

I didn't say they *did*. I said they *could*.

And also I'm sick.
I mean I'm getting sick right this second.
I mean my head hurts so much I can't see.

And my knee hurts so much I can't walk.
And my throat hurts so much I can't swallow
supper or water or anything except a little
chocolate chocolate chip ice cream.
I mean maybe I'm dying.

No I won't feel better soon.
I won't feel better ever.

You're still going?
Even though my temperature is probably a
hundred and eight or a hundred and ten?

Don't go.
Don't go until you read me one more book.
Okay, half a book.
A poem?

I'm really mad now.
I mean—mad!
I mean, tomorrow, when you say "Good morning,"
I'm not saying good morning.

And tomorrow, when you say "Guess who we met at the restaurant last night," I'm not guessing. And tomorrow, when you say "Let's read a book," I'm covering up my ears and I'm not listening.

Maybe I won't even be here.

Maybe I'll run away and find a new family that always stays home and never goes to French restaurants.

You're going to be so sad.
You're going to cry and cry.
You're going to be really sorry.

You're . . . going? You're still going to the restaurant?

Stop that. I don't want that.
I don't want a good-bye kiss.
I don't want to say good-bye.

I'm not saying good-bye.
I'll never say good-bye!

Good-bye.